Parents and Caregivers,

Stone Arch Readers are designed to provide enjoyable reading experiences, as well as opportunities to develop vocabulary, literacy skills, and comprehension. Here are a few ways to support your beginning reader:

○ Talk with your child about the ideas addressed in the story.

○ Discuss each illustration, mentioning the characters, where they are, and what they are doing.

○ Read with expression, pointing to each word. You may want to read the whole story through and then revisit parts of the story to ensure that the meanings of words or phrases are understood.

○ Talk about why the character did what he or she did and what your child would do in that situation.

○ Help your child connect with characters and events in the story.

Remember, reading with your child should be fun, not forced. Each moment spent reading with your child is a priceless investment in his or her literacy life.

Gail Saunders-Smith, Ph.D.

STONE ARCH READERS

are published by Stone Arch Books
a Capstone Imprint
151 Good Counsel Drive
P.O. Box 669
Mankato, Minnesota 56002
www.capstonepub.com

Library of Congress Cataloging-in-Publication data
is available on the Library of Congress website.
ISBN: 978-1-4342-2510-8 (library binding)
ISBN: 978-1-4342-3047-8 (paperback)

Summary: Gary is going to be a big brother.
Will Gary have a new sister or a new brother?

Reading Consultants:
Gail Saunders-Smith, Ph.D.
Melinda Melton Crow, M.Ed.
Laurie K. Holland, Media Specialist

Art Director/Designer: Kay Fraser
Production Specialist: Michelle Biedscheid

Printed in the United States of America in Stevens Point, Wisconsin.
010541R

illustrated by Andy Rowland

Little Lizard's
NEW BABY

by Melinda Melton Crow

STONE ARCH BOOKS
a capstone imprint

This is Dad Lizard.
This is Mom Lizard.
This is Gary Lizard.

Gary is going to be
a big brother.

Gary is happy.

"I will show him how to run,"
said Gary.

"Good," said Dad.

"I will show him how to jump," said Gary.

"Good," said Mom.

"I will show him how to ride a bike," said Gary.

"Good," said Dad.

"I will show him how to swim," said Gary.

"Good," said Mom.

"I will be good to my new
brother," said Gary.

"No. You will be good to your new sister," said Mom.

"A new sister? Hooray!"
said Gary.

STORY WORDS

Total Word Count: 100